I am going to read
All of

The Sleuths of Somerville

THE PROFESSOR'S DISCOVERY

The Sleuths of Somerville is published by Stone Arch Books
A Capstone Imprint
1710 Roe Crest Drive
North Mankato, MN 56003
www.mycapstone.com

Library of Congress Cataloging-in-Publication Data
Cataloging-in-publication information is on file with the Library
of Congress.
ISBN 978-1-4965-3177-3 (library binding)
ISBN 978-1-4965-3185-8 (eBook PDF)

"A history professor has made a startling discovery in the town of
Somerville. It sparks a mystery that needs solving. Quinn, Astrid,
Jace, and Rowan are on the case!"—Provided by publisher.

Designer: Tracy McCabe

Illustration Credits: Amerigo Pinelli

Printed and bound in China.
009744F16

The Sleuths of Somerville

THE PROFESSOR'S DISCOVERY

by Michele Jakubowski

STONE ARCH BOOKS
a capstone imprint

CHAPTER ONE

Rowan and Astrid Vega stood in front of the Somerville Cinema with their best friends, Quinn and Jace, blinking as their eyes adjusted to the bright sunshine.

"I'm going to have nightmares for weeks!" Astrid said.

"Are you kidding me? That was awesome! Don't be such a baby," replied her brother, Rowan.

At twelve, Rowan was only fourteen months older than his sister, but he took every opportunity to act superior.

Toward the end of a summer that had already had more than its fair share of excitement, a matinee movie was just what the foursome needed.

"I thought *Mutant Zombies from Outer Space Six* was better, but this one was pretty good, too," Jace said.

"I liked it, but I still don't understand how the zombies came back after their planet was blown up in the last movie," Quinn added.

"I can't explain that," Astrid said with a smile. "But I do know that I am hungry!"

"Are you serious? After you finished off that huge tub of popcorn?" Rowan asked.

Astrid rolled her eyes at her brother. "Whatever. Let's head back to the diner."

Mick's Diner was the best place to eat in Somerville, and it also happened to be owned by Astrid and Rowan's parents, Amelia and Jason Vega.

As the kids headed down Main Street, they saw a man, a woman, and two teenagers walking toward them. The man walked in front of the others and appeared to be thoroughly lost. He alternated between looking up at the street signs and down at a piece of paper in his hand.

With its location near Highway 84 and its small-town charm, Somerville got its fair share of tourists passing through. Most enjoyed a delicious meal at Mick's Diner and a walk down Main Street before filling up on cheap gas at Earl's Gas Station and getting back on the road.

As Rowan, Jace, Astrid, and Quinn got closer, they knew right away that these people were, indeed, a typical family of tourists. The man was tall and thin with disheveled, curly red hair and round wire glasses. The woman was small and stood with a stiff back as she clutched a oversized designer handbag with both hands. Large sunglasses and a puckered look decorated her face. The teenage boy and girl behind them wore bored expressions and well-made, expensive clothes. They had shoes that cost more than some folks in Somerville might have paid for their rent each month. Their phones were the latest models and brand-new.

"Hi, there," Rowan said in his friendliest voice. His parents had always reminded him to be nice to tourists, since they were so important to the success of Somerville's businesses. "Can we help you find something?"

Without looking up from the phone he was tapping away on, the teenage boy said, "How about a way out of this ridiculous little town?"

"Jefferson!" snapped the man. "There is no need to be rude."

"Whatever," the boy muttered without looking up as he shook his hair out of his face.

The man shot the teenage boy a look before turning toward Rowan. "We're actually looking for the Somerville Museum," he said. "Is it nearby?"

"It sure is," Astrid responded politely. "You're actually very close. It's just a few doors down past the movie theater and the Sugar Shack, on the right."

"It looks more like an old house than a big museum," Quinn said. "You have to keep an eye out for it. It's pretty easy to miss."

The Somerville Museum was located in one of the original houses built along Main Street. Its curator, Mrs. Ruth Partridge, displayed pieces of the town's history throughout the first floor and lived in a second-floor apartment with her beloved dog, Rex.

The tourist girl snapped her gum as she whined, "Daddy, you promised we could get some food if we went to the stupid museum. Find out where we can get some food. I'm hungry!"

"I will, Tabitha, and the museum is *not* stupid!" The man's face reddened as he spoke to the girl.

"You did promise them food, Harry," the woman said. "We've been in the car for hours. If we had just gone to Hawaii like I wanted to, everyone would have been much happier."

The man's face grew a frightening shade of red. Jace tried to help out, saying, "Mick's Diner has the best food in town! The museum is very close to here, and when you're done, the diner is back the other way, just before Highway 84."

The man took a few deep breaths, and his face slowly returned to its natural pale hue. He smiled at Jace, Rowan, Astrid, and Quinn and said, "You have been very helpful." The kids watched the man, his family trailing behind, walk down the street toward the museum.

Later at the diner, Mr. Vega listened with great interest as the kids told him all about the *Mutant Zombies from Outer Space 7* as they sat at the counter eating their grilled-cheese sandwiches.

"This one time Jake the Zombie Slayer attacked the head zombie and cut his head off!" Rowan said.

"Loads of blood squirted out everywhere!" Jace continued, waving his arms for dramatic effect. "But then, two heads popped out where the one had been!"

"Awesome!" said Mr. Vega.

"That's disgusting," said Mrs. Vega, frowning. "What was this movie rated? Are you sure it's appropriate for you guys?"

"It's fine, Mom!" Astrid said with a wave of her hand. She leaned forward and in a quieter voice added, "But I might want to sleep with you guys tonight."

They continued to tell Mr. Vega about the goriest parts of the movie. Soon the family that had been looking for the museum entered the diner.

The woman and the teenage kids still wore the same bored expressions, but the man was beaming as he made his way over to the counter.

"Thank you so much for your help!" he said as he clapped Rowan and Jace on the back.

"Welcome to Mick's Diner," Mr. Vega said warmly. "I'm glad the kids could be of some help. Uh . . . what did they do?"

The man shook his head. "Oh! I'm sorry! How rude of me! I'm Professor Harry Higgins," he said as he extended his hand to Mr. Vega. "These kids were most kind in helping me find your town's amazing museum."

"Amazing?" Mr. Vega asked as he shook Professor Higgins's hand. Obviously confused, he added, "The Somerville Museum?"

"Indeed!" the professor replied, beaming. He looked around the diner to make sure no one was listening before he leaned in and whispered, "I probably shouldn't be saying anything yet, but I may have just made a major historical discovery in your museum."

CHAPTER TWO

Professor Harry Higgins had a lot to say to his new acquaintances at the diner. While his family settled into a booth near the back, the professor shared with them how he had been in a bit of a rut. While he had enjoyed his job teaching in the History Department at Yale University, he had recently taken some time off from the classroom to work on a book. Unfortunately, the writing wasn't going very well.

Professor Higgins explained that his solution to this rut had been to take a cross-country road trip with his family. He was hoping the time together would bring them closer. He had also planned stops along the route to visit historical sites and museums to help him find inspiration for his book. They had been on the road for over a week, and the best thing Professor Higgins had found was a good pair of earplugs that blocked out his family's whining and complaining.

He said his luck was beginning to change, though. He felt overjoyed about the discovery he'd made at the Somerville Museum. His family did not share his enthusiasm, however, and he yearned to talk about his discovery with someone who might appreciate it.

The Vegas, Quinn, and Jace were definitely interested in hearing more about the discovery. They settled Professor Higgins's family at a table,

east as part of the western expansion. The ma

most instrumental in the town's founding

obviously, Albert J. Somer. Through

work and leadership, the town grew

and was a model for neighbo

developed. He made such

the people all agreed t

He stopped, loo

why am I te

know y

...e was too ...ted to eat, but once Mrs. Vega set a plate of mouth-watering food in front of him, he found he was famished. He swallowed a large bite of burger and began, saying, "As I'm sure you already know, Somerville was founded in 1860 by a group of pioneers who had traveled all the way from the was,

his hard

and prospered

ing towns as they

an impact, in fact, that

o name the town after him."

ed around, and chuckled. "But

ing you all this? I'm sure you already

ur town's history!"

Rowan, Astrid, Quinn, Jace, and Mr. and Mrs. Vega laughed nervously and avoided making eye contact with Professor Higgins. As proud as they were of their town, most of what they knew about its history came from folktales passed down from older residents rather than from documented facts.

Professor Higgins continued with a twinkle in his eye. "What you might not know is that Albert Somer was a childhood friend of Abraham Lincoln."

"You mean, as in sixteenth-President-of-the-United-States Abraham Lincoln?" asked Rowan.

"The one and only," said Professor Higgins, smiling. "The curator at the museum—was it Mrs. Rex?"

"Mrs. Ruth Partridge," Mrs. Vega said. "Rex is her dog."

"Yes! Mrs. Partridge, the dear woman. What a very friendly little dog! Anyway, she was most kind and let me poke through some boxes of things she didn't have on display. I was only a box or two in when I found something incredible!"

All six of them sat on the edge of their seats. Professor Higgins paused, as if for dramatic effect, but he couldn't contain himself for long.

"I found a letter President Lincoln had written to Albert Somer, wishing him well before he left for out West," he said.

Professor Higgins looked at his audience, and he seemed to understand that while they were impressed, they still didn't understand the importance or value of such a letter. They nodded and raised their eyebrows and murmured "cool" and "neat." This was not the level of enthusiasm he expected.

Professor Higgins sighed heavily and quickly added, "A similar letter recently sold at auction for one hundred and twenty-five thousand dollars."

He finally got the reaction he had been looking for since he'd made his find.

"What? Someone paid that much money for an old letter?" Rowan said.

"Holy cow! And it's been sitting in a box all these years?" Astrid said.

"That's crazy!" Quinn added.

Although he knew they were reacting to the monetary value more than the historical value, Professor Higgins enjoyed their reactions for a moment longer and then quieted them down. "We need to keep this to ourselves for a while. From what I gathered from Mrs. Partridge, the museum and all of its belongings are the property of the town and its residents. I still need to get the letter validated and do some more research before we can let anyone know. If word got out now, it may create some unnecessary drama. Once we know it's authentic, we can determine a way to tell the townspeople and decide how to proceed. I would strongly suggest donating the letter to a larger museum, where it can be seen and appreciated by many people."

No one heard Professor Higgins's suggestion, however. They were all excited about what the money might do for the town.

"I think we should build a shopping mall!" suggested Astrid.

"I think we should use that money to update the schools," said Mrs. Vega.

"What we need in Somerville is a mini-golf course!" Rowan said.

"What we *really* need is to keep this under wraps for the time being," Professor Higgins warned. "All three of you have very different ideas. Imagine if all the residents of Somerville knew about the potential windfall. It could lead to pandemonium!

What if the letter is a fake? If it's authentic, I'd love for the townspeople to be as excited about the letter's historical relevance and the pride it would bring your town as they are about the monetary value, but either way, we should keep quiet about it. I'll have Mrs. Partridge lock it up at the museum while I do some research. I'll be in touch soon."

They all realized that Professor Higgins was right about keeping the letter a secret. What they didn't realize was that Mrs. Arlene Studebaker, the town gossip, had been sitting quietly in the booth right behind them. She'd been listening the entire time.

CHAPTER THREE

Gossip in a small town works very much like a game of Telephone. One person tells a story to a friend, and that person tells another friend, and so on and so on. As in a game of Telephone, with each retelling, the gossip changes a bit, which can lead to peculiar results.

Arlene Studebaker had worked the counter at the Somerville Post Office for over thirty years.

She would never admit it, but what she loved most about her job was watching what people received in the mail and what they sent out. Mr. Mike Reynolds, the postmaster, had talked to Mrs. Studebaker several times about minding her own business, but she still kept an eye and ear out for juicy gossip.

Mrs. Studebaker could not believe her ears when she overheard the professor's news in Mick's Diner. She had heard the part about the importance of keeping it secret, but she figured there would be no harm in telling one person, her best friend, Ms. Patty Meyers. Ms. Meyers was Mayor Arnold's secretary and a very trustworthy friend. Ms. Meyers assumed there would be no problem in telling just one person—Mrs. Marge Goodwin, who owned Goodwin's Market with her husband. But Anthony Larsen in the meat department overheard the news, and he just had to impress his girlfriend, Kayla, with the story. And on and on it went. As the word spread, the part about not telling anyone got dropped. By the time it got back to Mrs. Vega at the diner, the story was that Abe Lincoln's famous stovepipe hat had been found in the basement of the museum. People said the town might get one million dollars for it.

Mrs. Vega told her husband what she had heard, and they immediately contacted Professor Higgins, who had been researching the letter in nearby Watertown. Together they spoke with Mayor Arnold and explained the situation. The mayor agreed that a town meeting was necessary to clear up the confusion.

Less than a week after Professor Higgins had first come to visit, he was back in Somerville, standing before the town's residents, who had gathered in the town square.

Rowan, Jace, Quinn, and Astrid were annoyed that the gossip had been spread. It had been exciting when they were the only ones who knew. The fact that the story had gotten so messed up made it even worse.

Rowan went so far as to accuse Astrid of leaking the news.

"Who would I have told?" she argued. "Everyone I would have shared it with was sitting at the table when Professor Higgins told us!"

They stood at the back with their arms folded as Professor Higgins addressed the crowd.

"Thank you all for coming today," he began. "My name is Harry Higgins. I have been a professor of U.S. history at Yale for more than twenty years."

A murmur of approval went through the crowd, and the people, finally interested, gave Professor Higgins their full attention.

"I know some stories have been circulating through Somerville in regards to an historical find I made in the town's museum," he said. "While most of the information that has been going around is false, I can confirm today that some of it is true."

A buzz of excitement passed through the crowd as the people of Somerville all hoped that the part of the story about one million dollars was the truth. Professor Higgins assumed that their excitement was due to his credentials and his significant historical revelation. He relaxed a bit and began to enjoy himself in front of the eager crowd. He hadn't felt this appreciated in front of a group in a long time. Recently his students had seemed downright bored in his lectures.

"I made a great discovery at your museum that will go down in presidential history!" he continued in a louder, more enthusiastic voice. He went on to remind the townspeople of the history of their town, and when he felt as though he was losing their attention he jumped straight to the good part: "And buried deep in a box tucked away at the museum I found a personal letter written to Albert J. Somer from his dear boyhood friend, the one and only Abraham Lincoln!"

He paused and scanned the crowd to gauge their reaction. A few people in the crowd wore stunned expressions, while the majority of them looked confused. A letter wasn't nearly as exciting as Abraham Lincoln's stovepipe hat. How much could a letter be worth, anyway?

"So we're not getting a million dollars?" asked Marcus Sloane, manager at Earl's Gas Station.

"No, you will not be getting a million dollars," Professor Higgins said. "But," he added quickly, "I can tell you that I've spent the past few days doing some research and can confirm that the letter is authentic. Such letters are rare, and this one is in excellent condition. It is beautifully written and a quite personal and charming look into the friendship shared by these two men."

The crowd remained silent for a moment as people absorbed the news. Finally someone yelled what many people were wondering: "How much is it worth?"

Professor Higgins slumped his shoulders in frustration. He had hoped that the people of Somerville would appreciate the historic importance of the letter. His worst fear had come to fruition when he realized that all they cared about was the money.

"That has yet to be determined," he said in a tight voice. The crowd began to grumble. They were not going to let the professor get away with such a vague answer. The crowd shifted closer to him and demanded a more solid answer.

After more questions that he felt he couldn't explain well enough, the professor finally gave up any hope that the townspeople would be satisfied with the letter's historical value and told the boisterous crowd, "The letter is valued at between seventy-five to one hundred twenty-five thousand dollars!"

The professor closed his eyes and braced himself. He knew what was coming. Unfortunately, the crowd acted much like he had predicted. Even though it wasn't the million dollars some had anticipated, the townspeople all had big plans for the money. The pandemonium began.

CHAPTER FOUR

The residents of Somerville quickly divided into groups based on what they thought should be done with the money. No one seemed to think the museum should keep the letter. No one seemed to care that it had belonged to the person who founded their town.

The largest group was led by Mr. Lance Varner. Word of the letter had spread to Watertown, where

Mr. Varner was a successful businessman. He dabbled in several businesses but made most of his money from Wave Kingdom, the water park he owned in Watertown. Many of the tourists who passed through Somerville were on their way to Wave Kingdom. And since Watertown was only 30 miles down the highway, many Somerville residents also enjoyed its slides, wave pool, lazy river, and splash pad each summer.

From the minute he'd heard about the letter and its potential worth, Lance Varner couldn't wait to share the perfect investment opportunity for the people of Somerville: Wave Kingdom Jr.

"It will be a smaller version of Wave Kingdom located right here in Somerville!" he'd told the crowd that had gathered at Mick's Diner to hear him pitch his idea. "You won't have to drive all the way to Watertown anymore, and think of all the visitors it will bring to your local businesses!"

As he said this last part, he winked at Mrs. Vega and flashed a big, toothy smile. Instead of being interested in a plan that might bring more business to the diner, though, Mrs. Vega felt a little shiver run down her spine. She had a gut feeling that Lance Varner couldn't be trusted.

"I don't know about this," she whispered to the woman next to her, Mrs. Coretta Lownie. Miss Coco, as the oldest living resident of Somerville was known, would definitely have an opinion.

And she did. "No kidding," Miss Coco replied. "Water parks should only be located in towns that have *water* in their name. Everyone knows that! It's much safer that way."

Mrs. Vega smiled, as she was used to Miss Coco's often-wacky comments.

"Besides," Miss Coco went on, "why would we need two water parks so close to each other? Wouldn't they be competing for business?"

Miss Coco's clarity on the situation surprised Mrs. Vega. She turned her head slowly toward the old woman, wondering why she hadn't thought of that herself.

Mrs. Vega stood up and got Mr. Varner's attention. She repeated Miss Coco's question.

The wide smile fell from Mr. Varner's face for a brief moment. It reappeared as he said, "There's plenty of business for everyone! Who doesn't love a water park?"

The crowd cheered, and no one was cheering louder than Jace, Quinn, Astrid, and Rowan. They loved the idea of Wave Kingdom Jr. A water park so close to home? Finally there would be something fun to do in Somerville! The local business owners were also thrilled with the prospect of more traffic through town.

Mr. Varner went on to tell the eager crowd that they needed to act fast to make sure Wave Kingdom Jr. happened. He explained that other investors were anxious to get things moving, and that work on the water park needed to start right away.

Mrs. Vega spoke up one more time. "But we don't even know how much money we'll get from the letter, if any at all. Should we start spending the money before we know if we'll even get it? That seems irresponsible."

Mr. Varner seemed to have lost his patience with Mrs. Vega. His smile looked forced as he said, "Oh, we'll get the money. I'll make sure of it."

For the second time that afternoon, Mrs. Vega felt a shiver run down her spine.

CHAPTER FIVE

Astrid and Rowan could not stop thinking about Wave Kingdom Jr.

"We'll be able to walk to a water park every day!" Astrid gushed as she imagined herself spending entire afternoons floating around the lazy river.

"I hope they have cool slides," Rowan added. "I heard Mr. Varner tell someone that it would be no problem for us to get a Super Duper Looper like Watertown has!"

Mr. Vega had sent the siblings to the post office to pick up some stamps and send out a package. They were so lost in their daydreams about Wave Kingdom Jr. they didn't even mind waiting in line as Mrs. Studebaker stood and chatted with Mrs. Singh, who had long since finished her transaction.

Astrid and Rowan were so lost in their thoughts that it took a moment before they realized what the two ladies were discussing.

"You didn't hear it from me," Mrs. Studebaker said in a voice loud enough for anyone in the post office to hear, "but I think Captain Osgood might be up to something."

Mrs. Singh's eyes grew wide. "What on earth could Captain Osgood possibly be up to? He's such a good man!"

Mrs. Studebaker held up her hands and quickly said, "Oh, I'm not saying he's up to no good. I mean, he may be. Who am I to say? What I do know is that he's been sending out a lot of packages lately. I mean *a lot*! When I asked him about it, he said he's been selling things in online auctions. He claimed he needed the money for something but wouldn't tell me for what."

Mrs. Singh frowned and nodded, unsure of what Mrs. Studebaker was implying.

When she didn't respond, Mrs. Studebaker went on. "Kind of makes you wonder where he's getting the stuff to sell and why he needs the money, doesn't it?"

Mrs. Singh liked casual gossip, but she didn't like where this conversation was going. She looked relieved when she noticed Rowan and Astrid. "Well, looks like you've got more customers," she said, and she hurried out of the post office, leaving Rowan and Astrid to finish their business.

When the Vegas returned from the post office, their father told them their mom needed help.

"I can't wait for the water park to open," Astrid grumbled. "Then we won't be around to help around here all the time. They'll have to find someone else to do all their dirty work."

They found their mom in the meeting room located off the diner's main dining room. The room was rapidly filling up with people. Mrs. Vega looked relieved to see them and immediately put them to work.

As they began pouring lemonade and handing out pastries they realized that the group using the meeting room was the Somerville PTA, an organization of parents who had children in the Somerville school system.

"Thank you all for coming," Mrs. Vega said as she got the group's attention. "I know we don't usually meet in the summer, but I thought this was a topic too important to wait to discuss. I'm sure you've all heard by now about the letter Professor Higgings found, and the potential amount of money it may bring into the community. I know a lot of you may be excited about the idea of a water park, but I want you to think of what some of that money could mean to our schools and our children. We could use this money for something responsible."

The room fell silent. Rowan and Astrid watched the parents stop eating and drinking as Mrs. Vega's words sunk in. Many people in the room frowned in dismay, conflicted between wanting a local water park and choosing what was best for their children's education.

"Is she serious?" Rowan hissed at Astrid.

"If Somerville doesn't get Wave Kingdom Jr. because of our mom, we might as well change our names and move," Astrid responded. "Every kid in town will hate us."

As Mrs. Vega went on to list the ways in which the money could be spent on the schools, the parents began nodding and smiling. As much as a water park sounded fun, a better education for their children sounded better.

One parent, Stacy Halper, threw her arms up in excitement. Stacy had five children all under the age of six. She devoted her whole life to her children and volunteered for everything she could fit into her hectic schedule.

"My goodness!" she exclaimed loudly, drawing the group's attention away from Mrs. Vega and toward herself. "This is so briliant I'm surprised I didn't think of it first!"

"Thanks, Stacy," Mrs. Vega smiled, a bit taken aback by Mrs. Halper's outburst. After a moment she went on. "Now, I'm not suggesting we use all the money for the schools. There are plenty of other projects around town that chould also benefit from the find. But even a small percentage would make a big difference to our children."

"No!" shouted Mrs. Halper, startling everyone again. She had found her way to take over Mrs. Vega's idea. "I think we need all the money! Who's more important in this town than our children?"

Mrs. Vega tried to calm Mrs. Halper down by speaking in a slow and quiet voice. "That I completely agree with, Stacy, but there are plenty of things that can be done with some of the money that would help others in the community who need it, too."

"Yeah," Rowan whispered to Astrid, "like build a water park."

"No!" Mrs. Halper shouted even louder this time. She had the wild look of someone who had chugged one too many energy drinks. "I think we should make it our mission to make sure every penny of that money goes to our children! Who's with me?"

Rowan and Astrid exchanged wide-eyed looks that said, *Is this lady going crazy?*

Mrs. Vega realized she was losing control of the meeting. She tried to settle Mrs. Halper down. "We don't even know if we'll be getting *any* money."

"I'll make sure we get it!" Mrs. Halper promised the crowd. She seemed to love the fact that everyones' eyes were on her. She added, "I won't rest until we do!"

"Why don't we think about it some more?" Mrs. Vega said. "How does that sound?"

"Yes! I'll set up a meeting and send out invitations!" Mrs. Halper said. "I'll begin forming committees and doing research!"

As Mrs. Halper went on, the stunned parents nodded and went back to eating and drinking.

Mrs. Vega walked over to her children and grabbed a glass of lemonade. In a low voice she muttered, "Geez, you try to do a good thing . . ."

Astrid and Rowan nodded as if they agreed, but they were really relieved that her plan to stop the water park wasn't going very well. As soon as she walked away, the kids quietly high-fived.

CHAPTER SIX

A few mornings later, when Mr. Vega went to unlock the front door of the diner, he found Miss Coco waiting outside.

"Oh! Good morning, Miss Coco! You startled me," he said as he held the door for her. "What brings you in so early?"

Miss Coco look flustered. Her hair, which was normally pulled back in a neat bun, was a mess today. And Mr. Vega noticed she was still wearing her fuzzy pink slippers.

"I couldn't sleep!" she told him. "This whole letter business has made a mess out of me!"

Mrs. Vega and Evie were at the counter, setting out fresh baked goods for display. Rowan, Astrid, and Jace sat at a table nearby, rolling silverware into napkins.

"Good morning, Miss Coco! You're here bright and early," Evie said. Evie was Jace's sister, and she'd taken a job at the diner soon after the two arrived in town.

"Well, hello." Miss Coco looked embarrassed as she tried to tidy her hair. She extended her hand to Evie. "It's nice to meet you, dear. I'm Mrs. Coretta Lownie. Welcome to Somerville."

"I know," Evie began, but gave up. She had been in Somerville for over two months, and she had waited on Miss Coco at the diner almost daily. For some reason the old woman could never remember her.

Mrs. Vega smiled at Evie and suppressed a laugh as she poured Miss Coco a cup of coffee. "Everything okay, Miss Coco?"

"Oh, I don't know," she sighed as she began pouring sugar into her cup. "This whole letter thing has the town acting crazy. Something needed to be done."

She went on. "Reminds me of the time Old Man Watson found some gold while digging in his garden. Sent the whole town into a tizzy! Everyone became convinced they were living on a gold mine and began digging up their own land. By the time Mrs. Watson admitted that she was planning to leave Old Man Watson, and had been burying gold around the yard to take with her, most of Somerville had been dug up!"

"Rumor had it that Mr. Brown was so convinced there was gold to be had that he dug straight through to China and was never heard from again. Poor man." Miss Coco thought for a moment before continuing her story. "Although if I remember correctly, he was a fan of Chinese food, so I guess it all worked out for the best."

Mrs. Vega noticed Miss Coco was still pouring sugar into her cup, so she slowly reached over and stopped her. Nobody could want that much sugar, she knew. "I agree, Miss Coco," she said. "Things have gotten out of control around here."

In the past couple of days, Mrs. Vega's plan to make some updates to the schools had become an all-out obsession for Stacy Halper. She was bound and determined to make sure all of the money went to the schools and that she was going to be the one responsible for taking care of it.

As if she could read what was on Mrs. Vega's mind, Evie asked, "Did you see that Stacy Halper started a petition to ensure that any money from the sale of the letter goes to the school? She's got people going door to door for signatures and putting signs in their yards."

"Yeah, and I heard that Lance Varner got a hold of that information and is ramping up his sales pitch for the water park," Mr. Vega added. "He told people that if they were interested, they need to begin investing their own money now so they can be sure to have enough when the letter is sold at auction."

"That's ridiculous," Mrs. Vega argued. "Why would anyone give him money now, when no one has agreed to use the money from the letter for a water park?"

"This whole thing is ridiculous!" Miss Coco exclaimed. "A little bit of money and this town is willing to sell its history. It's disgraceful!"

Everyone stopped what they were doing and looked at Miss Coco. It somehow seemed fitting that the woman whom some people lovingly called Miss Cuckoo was now the voice of reason in a town full of crazy people.

Miss Coco took a sip of her coffee and wrinkled her nose in disgust. She waved at Evie and said, "Excuse me, dear? Can you please get me another cup of coffee? You made this one too sweet!"

Without saying a word, Evie smiled and took away Miss Coco's coffee and brought her a new cup. As she filled it with coffee, Miss Coco asked, "Are you new here, dear?"

The smile disappeared from Evie's face, but before she could introduce herself to Miss Coco for the umpteenth time, the diner's door banged open. Mrs. Ruth Partridge burst in and shouted hysterically, "The letter has been stolen!"

CHAPTER SEVEN

Shortly after Mrs. Partridge's arrival, the diner began filling up with the breakfast crowd. Instead of causing a town riot by discussing the news of the missing letter, Mr. Vega called Captain Joel Osgood of the Somerville Police. Mrs. Vega settled down Mrs. Partridge with a cinnamon roll and a cup of coffee. Captain Osgood said he would meet Mrs. Partridge back at the museum. Mrs. Vega insisted that Rowan, Jace, and Astrid walk her there.

As they approached the museum, they saw a sleepy-looking Quinn waiting out front. Before leaving the diner, Astrid had quickly called Quinn and woke her up, saying, "Big news! Meet me at the museum!"

"What is going on?" Quinn asked as her friends approached. "I was beginning to think I'd dreamt your call."

"Dream? It's more like a nightmare!" Mrs. Partridge said.

Just then Captain Osgood arrived and got out of his police car. He was all business as he glanced up and down the street before saying, "Let's go inside."

Inside the museum, several display cases filled the floor, and old photographs and documents hung on the wall. Town artifacts ranging from a small ticket stub from the first movie shown at the Somerville Cinema to a wheel from one of the original stagecoaches ridden by the settlers were displayed proudly. Mrs. Partridge took her job as curator very seriously. Her museum showcased pieces of history from the town's founding straight through to modern-day accomplishments.

The museum looked as neat and organized as it always did. It was hard to believe there had been a burglary. Caption Osgood reminded everyone not to touch a thing and then began asking Mrs. Partridge what had happened.

"Well," Mrs. Partridge took a deep breath and began her story, "I came downstairs to take Rex out to do his morning business. I usually take the back stairs out of my apartment, but a mama bunny and her babies have moved into the yard, and Rex goes crazy when he sees them. I don't think Rex would hurt them. He just wants to play. But I would feel just awful if anything happened to the bunnies. They are just the cutest little things!"

Quinn leaned over and whispered to Astrid, "You woke me up to hear about some baby bunnies in Mrs. Partridge's yard?"

Astrid shushed Quinn. Mrs. Partridge continued her story. "Anyway, I was walking through the museum toward the front door, and I noticed right away that the safe where I kept the letter was wide open and the letter was missing."

Quinn gasped, and Astrid nodded, a smile of satisfaction on her face. "Worth getting up for, wasn't it?" she said.

Mrs. Partridge added, "I've looked everywhere. It's gone!"

"Why was the letter being kept here?" Captain Osgood asked. "I assumed Professor Higgins would have it?"

"He got so frustrated with all the fighting about the money that he flew to Hawaii to meet up with his family. Said he'd be back in a few weeks and hoped we'd have it sorted out by then," Mrs. Partridge explained. "He didn't want to take the letter with him, and we agreed it would be safest locked up here at the museum. At least we thought it would be!"

The kids stood in silence as Captain Osgood searched around the museum. When he was done with his inspection, he frowned and said, "Well, there's no sign of a forced entry into the building, and whoever stole the letter knew the combination for the safe."

"Everyone in town's been snooping around here since the letter was found," Mrs. Partridge said with a sigh. "But I'm sure I didn't give that combination to anyone."

"There are plenty of suspects," Rowan said.

"Everyone in town wanted that money for one reason or another," Jace agreed.

Captain Osgood looked at the boys as if he'd just noticed they were there. "You kids should get going," he said abruptly.

"Why?" Rowan asked. "We want to help you find the letter!"

The captain shook his head, opened the front door, and said, "I appreciate the offer, but it's not a good idea."

When it was clear that Captain Osgood wasn't going to change his mind, Rowan, Jace, Quinn, and Astrid walked slowly out the museum's door.

Stunned, they headed down the street aimlessly, their frustration clear.

"What was that all about?" Rowan asked, walking quickly ahead of the others.

Quinn crossed her arms tightly and frowned. "He didn't mind our help with those creepy bike race guys. How quickly people forget!"

"And we're the ones who found Mrs. Partridge's dog!" Jace added.

"All of a sudden the captain does not want our help," Astrid said. "Why?"

Rowan stopped suddenly, causing Jace, Quinn, and Astrid to knock into each other like dominoes.

"Hey!" Astrid called. She didn't enjoy being jostled between Jace and Quinn.

Rowan pointed at his sister, and she braced herself to be yelled at about something. Instead he asked in a low voice, "Do you remember what we heard Mrs. Studebaker say to Mrs. Singh at the post office?"

Astrid tried to remember. Her voice uncertain, she guessed: "That she thought the butcher was putting his thumb on the scale at the market and overcharging her for lunch meat?"

"No!" Rowan shook his head in annoyance. "The part about Captain Osgood, remember? How he's been selling stuff online and being mysterious about it?"

Astrid's eyes grew wide as she remembered. "You don't think Captain Osgood stole the letter to sell it online, do you?"

"It doesn't seem like something he'd do," Rowan said with a shrug. "But why else would he be so quick to throw us out of there?"

The four friends stood on the sidewalk in silence. They knew that if they suspected someone of stealing, they should go to the police. What they didn't know was whom to go to when they suspected the police.

CHAPTER EIGHT

"We need to call Mr. P.," Rowan said in his most certain voice. "He'll be able to help us find out if Captain Osgood had anything to do with the stolen letter."

The foursome had convened back at the old Potters' place, which was now Jace and Evie's house on the outskirts of Somerville. They had been sitting around the kitchen island and debating what to do next, since Captain Osgood had kicked them out of the Somerville Museum.

"We *cannot* call Mr. P.," Jace replied. "He'll tell us this is a dangerous situation and that we need to stay out of it. He might even make Evie and me leave if he thinks Captain Osgood is up to no good. He's supposed to be one of the people keeping us safe in Somerville!"

Mr. P. was the special agent responsible for Jace and Evie while their parents were in hiding. He didn't tend to show a lot of emotion, and he took his job very seriously. Even though Astrid referred to him as an "odd duck," they had all grown to like him and his quirky ways.

"Then what can we do?" Quinn asked. They agreed that they needed to help find the letter. There was no way they could sit around and do nothing.

Astrid sighed. "I don't know. I just can't believe Captain Osgood had anything to do with the letter disappearing," she said. "He's such a good guy!"

Rowan frowned and replied, "I know, but I keep remembering what Mrs. Studebaker said. She thought it was suspicious that Captain Osgood wouldn't tell her what he was selling and why he needed the money. You have to admit that does sound kind of strange. Captain Osgood is not the type to keep secrets."

"Plus, if he needs a lot of money fast, selling that letter would certainly do the trick," Jace added.

They were all quiet for a moment.

"Although," Quinn said, sitting up straighter, "there could be plenty of other suspects besides Captain Osgood."

They all perked up. No one wanted to believe that Captain Osgood had anything to do with stealing the letter. It would be great if they could pin the crime on someone else.

"Everyone heard Mr. Varner promise that he'd get the money for the water park," Jace reminded them. "Do you think he's desperate enough to steal the letter to get it?"

"Maybe," Astrid nodded her head in agreement. She stood up and began pacing as she spoke. "And what about Mrs. Halper? She sounded like she'd do just about anything to get the money from the letter for the schools."

"She'll do anything it takes to help the schools. That's for sure," Rowan agreed. "Mrs. Halper once talked me into buying oatmeal raisin cookies at the school bake sale. I hate oatmeal raisin cookies, but I bought them anyway!"

"Sounds like we've got some leads," Jace said. "But Captain Osgood doesn't want us involved for some reason. How are we supposed to gather clues without getting in trouble?"

They sat, yet again, in frustrated silence.

"How about this?" Rowan said carefully. "Let's go see Captain Osgood one more time and try to find out what's going on. If we still think he might be involved in this, we'll call Mr. P. for help."

Jace began to protest, but Rowan held up a hand to interrupt him. "I don't think Captain Osgood is crooked, but if he is and we don't tell Mr. P., we'll all be in big trouble!"

Jace sighed. He couldn't argue with that. Their love of solving mysteries had put them in harm's way before, and he knew they'd be in big trouble with their parents and Mr. P. if it happened again.

Then the foursome made a plan and headed back to the Somerville Museum. They all hoped to be able to take Captain Osgood off the list of suspects.

CHAPTER NINE

If Captain Osgood was surprised to see them back at the museum, he didn't show it. He finished up giving orders to a police officer before addressing the kids.

"I thought I told you four to stay away from here," he said, a slight smile on his face.

The group had decided that Rowan would do all the talking. Their plan was to ask some direct questions to determine if Captain Osgood had anything to do with the letter's disappearance. They felt confident knowing they had Mr. P. on their side if they suspected Captain Osgood of any wrongdoing.

As Rowan opened his mouth to talk, he noticed someone enter the room from the back of the museum.

"Mr. P.?" Rowan said, unable to keep the surprise off his face.

"Good morning, children," Mr. P. said solemnly. "Actually," he amended, looking at his watch, "Good afternoon. It's 12:03 p.m."

Astrid especially enjoyed Mr. P.'s quirkiness. She tried to hold back a laugh as she asked, "Any idea what the temperature is?"

Without missing a beat, Mr. P. replied, "The current local temperature in Somerville is a sunny 83 degrees Fahrenheit."

Although it was a warm summer day, Mr. P. wore a dark suit with a crisp white shirt and black tie. Mr. P. was not one to smile very often, but the kids all found him amusing in his own way. It was hard to believe that Rowan, Astrid, and Quinn had been so afraid of Mr. P. when he'd first come to town.

Jace, who had known Mr. P. the longest and was used to his odd ways, said, "Well, now that we've got that cleared up, do you want to tell us why you're here, Mr. P.?"

Captain Osgood excused the officer who had been dusting for fingerprints before saying, "I called him."

"Why?" Rowan, Astrid, Quinn, and Jace all asked at the same time.

"When a valuable item is stolen, I consider that a potentially dangerous situation. That's why I told you all to go home," Captain Osgood said. "I also knew you four junior detectives wouldn't stay away, so I called Mr. P. in to assess the situation."

Rowan, Jace, Astrid, and Quinn were stunned. If Captain Osgood had stolen the letter, would he really call in a special agent from the National Intelligence Agency to investigate?

"So, uh, have you, uh, found out anything?" Rowan asked.

"It's a local job," Mr. P. said in a bored voice as he picked a piece of lint off his jacket. "There is no connection to your parents, Jace, and I don't feel you are in any great danger. My guess is someone is just trying to cash in on the professor's find. Whoever it is will have a very hard time doing that without getting caught."

"Someone local?" Quinn asked as she glanced tentatively in Captain Osgood's direction.

"Most definitely," Mr. P. replied. If he'd noticed Quinn's glance, he didn't show it. "I'm sure you'll be able to apprehend the perpetrator in no time."

"You're not going to help?" Rowan asked. Without Mr. P., they'd have to determine fairly quickly if the captain was a suspect or not.

Mr. P. shook his head. "If you need me, you know how to find me."

Captain Osgood spoke up. "I appreciate you taking a look, Mr. P. I know you've got more important things to take care of, so we won't take up any more of your time."

The foursome exchanged glances as Captain Osgood escorted Mr. P. toward the door. While they all knew it was unlikely that the captain was involved with stealing the letter, they had been hoping for Mr. P.'s help to rule him out altogether.

In a moment of desperation, Astrid blurted out, "Captain Osgood's been selling things online!"

Captain Osgood and Mr. P., who were halfway to the museum's door, stopped abruptly and turned around to look at Astrid. Rowan smacked himself on the forehead, and Jace and Quinn were frozen in shock.

"What are you implying?" Mr. P. asked, with caution in his voice.

Astrid felt her face grow warm and realized her cheeks were getting red with embarassment. She looked toward the others for help, but they stood staring back at her. "Nothing, I just, um, thought you should know."

"Yeah," Quinn finally spoke up. "In case that sort of thing might be important, or something, in the investigation."

"You think I stole the letter to sell online? How did you even know about—" Captain Osgood stopped talking, shook his head, and smiled. "Oh, wait, let me guess. Mrs. Studebaker told you I've been mailing things all over the place. Am I right?"

Astrid immediately felt guilty for accusing the captain. She looked at the ground as she nodded.

Mr. P. crossed his arms across his chest. "Does someone want to tell me what is going on here?"

Captain Osgood chuckled as he held up his hands in surrender. "It's true, I've been selling things online to save up some money. That doesn't mean I would steal anything."

"Sorry," Astrid mumbled.

"That's actually pretty good detective work," Captain Osgood said, looking impressed. "I could see where I'd be a suspect in your eyes. There was no forced entry, and someone in my field could have easily found a way in without being noticed."

Jace asked quietly, "Did you?"

"No," the captain said firmly but without anger. He looked a little embarrassed as he added, "I've been selling off my baseball card collection to save up for something, um, special."

He shot a quick look in Astrid and Quinn's direction. When the two didn't understand, Captain Osgood went on. "A certain piece of jewelry, for someone special . . ."

It was Mr. P. who announced what the captain was trying to say. "An engagement ring for Ms. Doherty," he clarified.

Rowan and Jace were still confused, but Astrid and Quinn caught on. They were the only ones who knew that Captain Osgood was secretly dating Delilah Doherty, the owner of the Sugar Shack. Or at least they thought they were the only ones who knew.

"How did you know?" Astrid asked Mr. P.

"I know everything," Mr. P. said dismissively. He turned toward Captain Osgood and said simply, "Congratulations."

"Would someone like to fill us in?" Rowan asked impatiently. He did not like to be out of the loop.

"Delilah and I have been dating for a while now. Quinn and Astrid saw us together once and promised not to say anything," Captain Osgood said. "Delilah's parents are always pressuring her to get married, so we wanted to keep things quiet as we got to know each other. She has no idea that I've been saving up for a ring."

The captain turned toward Mr. P. "I'm impressed that you figured it out. I thought we'd been good about keeping things quiet."

"Don't be. It's my job to know what's going on," Mr. P. said. "Now it's your job to find that letter. Mark my words, it's someone local."

Then Mr. P. got up. He left the museum without saying goodbye.

"I'm sorry we suspected you," Astrid mumbled to Captain Osgood.

"It's okay. I understand," Captain Osgood said. "Please don't say anything to Delilah about the ring. I want to surprise her."

"No problem," Astrid smiled, relieved that the captain was no longer a suspect and not mad at them for accusing him.

"Now, let's get to work finding our thief," the captain said.

"So, we can help you?" Jace asked hopefully.

"Sure," the captain smiled. "Mr. P. doesn't think the thief is dangerous, nor do I, but it's still a good idea to keep you guys close by while we find the letter. Plus, how could I leave out my best detectives?"

The four friends smiled, happy to be a part of the investigation again.

CHAPTER TEN

Two days had passed since Mrs. Partridge had reported the letter missing. So far they had been able to keep the news from spreading around town. Captain Osgood suggested, and the others agreed, that this information should be kept quiet during the investigation. Considering the pandemonium that had ensued after the letter's discovery, they could only imagine what would happen if the people of Somerville knew it had been stolen.

"Is it just me, or does the air smell fresher and the sun feel sunnier today?" Miss Coco beamed as she sat down at the counter at Mick's.

"My, aren't you in a good mood," Mrs. Vega commented as she poured a cup of coffee for Miss Coco.

"All just feels right in the world," Miss Coco responded. "Speaking of things that are right in the world, how about you get me two donuts with extra sprinkles?"

Jace and Rowan came into the diner and up to the counter as Mrs. Vega set out a tray of donuts.

"Don't mind if I do!" Rowan said, snatching up a red velvet donut with cream cheese frosting.

"You're lucky that wasn't one with sprinkles," Miss Coco told him. Rowan smiled at her, not quite sure if she was teasing or not.

Rowan took a huge bite and looked around to make sure no one was listening, before telling his mom in a quiet voice, "We're going to be upstairs working on you-know-what."

"Does 'you-know-what' involve you learning some manners and not talking with your mouth full?" Mrs. Vega responded.

"Sorry," Rowan said sheepishly.

Mrs. Vega smiled. "Astrid and Quinn are already upstairs waiting for you two. Why don't you bring them up a couple of donuts, too?"

"Not the ones with sprinkles!" Miss Coco warned.

Jace and Rowan found Astrid and Quinn in the living room. Astrid had taken out the dry-erase board she used to use when she and Quinn would play school. Across the top she had written "THE CASE OF THE MISSING LETTER" in a rainbow of colors. Underneath she had written "Suspects," and below that were two names—"Mr. Varner" and "Mrs. Halper." Initially she had listed Captain Osgood's name, but now she'd crossed it out.

"I've got one more name for you to add," Rowan told her as he set down the plate of donuts.

"Really?" Astrid asked as she reached for a different-colored marker. "Who?"

"Some guy named Dr. Whitaker," Jace said. He and Rowan had just been to see Captain Osgood to find out if there was any new information on the investigation. "He works at Watertown University in the History Department."

Rowan went on to explain how the fingerprints found at the museum were mostly those of locals who had been in recently, but that the police had also found prints from Dr. Whitaker.

"I heard that Mrs. Partridge went to stay with her sister-in-law in Seattle for a while. She said she couldn't take the pressure of not telling anyone that the letter was missing, plus she felt so guilty about its disappearance," Rowan explained. "But before she left, Captain Osgood asked her to come to the st ation. He asked her about all the people whose fingerprints had turned up. She said Dr.

Whitaker had been visiting a lot since Professor Higgins found the letter."

"According to Mrs. Partridge, he was 'quite a curmudgeon,'" Jace added.

"What the heck is a curmudgeon?" Quinn asked.

Jace laughed. "I guess he was a big grump! Mrs. Partridge said he came to the museum several times. He was really rude and asked a lot of questions."

Astrid used her green marker and added Dr. Whitaker's name to the list. She then stood back and looked at her work with her hands on her hips and a satisfied look on her face.

"Are you done coloring yet?" Rowan asked sarcastically.

"Hey!" Astrid replied. "Organization is an important part of any investigation."

Jace stepped between them before another brother-sister battle could begin. "Captain Osgood said Rowan and I could go with him when he goes to interview Dr. Whitaker tomorrow," he said.

"But he thought it would look weird if all four of us went."

"That's okay," Astrid said as she used her pointer to tap on Mrs. Halper's name. "We're going to interview suspect number two."

Rowan and Jace looked confused, so Quinn explained. "My mom told me that Mrs. Halper is always looking for help with her kids, especially in the summer. Astrid and I volunteered to help her tomorrow. We thought we could look for clues while we're there."

"That's a great idea," Jace said.

"Although I think you guys got the better assignment. Interviewing a rude guy sounds much easier than hanging out with all those Halper kids!" Astrid laughed.

Mrs. Vega walked in, carrying a tray with glasses and a pitcher of lemonade.

"How's the investigation going?" she asked.

Rowan opened his mouth to answer her, but quickly remembered it was full of donut.

"Great!" Astrid told her.

After she set down the tray, Mrs. Vega pulled a newspaper out from the front pocket of her apron.

"I thought you might want to see this." She handed Jace the paper. "It involves one of your suspects. I'm sure he already knows, but make sure Captain Osgood sees this."

As Jace scanned the front of the newspaper, his eyes grew wide. Quinn, Rowan, and Astrid, on the other hand, grew impatient.

"What does it say?" Astrid asked.

Rowan tried to get a look at what Jace was reading. "Which suspect?" he asked.

Jace flipped the paper around to show them the article. The headline read: "Varner Finds Anonymous Donor, Plans for Water Park Proceed."

"What does that mean?" Quinn asked.

Jace explained, "It says a person who wishes to remain anonymous donated a large amount of money to the water park. Mr. Varner said the donor is anxious to get started, but the people of

Somerville need to commit the money from the letter to the water park or the donor will take back his donation."

"Do you think the mystery donor stole the letter?" Astrid asked.

"Maybe," Rowan replied. "Why else would someone who is donating to a water park not want to be discovered?"

"Whoever it is, Mr. Varner must know who the person is," Jace pointed out.

"Should we cross Mr. Varner off the list and add 'Anonymous Donor'?" Astrid asked as she began searching for the right color of marker.

Rowan thought for a moment and then picked up a marker. Before Astrid could protest, he wrote on the board: "Mr. Varner = Anonymous Donor?"

CHAPTER ELEVEN

"Oh, thank you so much for coming!" Mrs. Halper looked haggard as she opened the front door. Although it was almost lunchtime, she wore pajamas, and her hair in a messy ponytail. She held a baby on each hip.

"This is Ella, and this is Emma," she said as she handed off one of the babies to Astrid and the other to Quinn. "No, wait, that's Emma, and that's Ella."

She paused, tilted her head, and squinted at the babies before mumbling, "I'm pretty sure."

Astrid and Quinn looked at the identical twins they were holding, impressed that Mrs. Halper managed to tell them apart at all.

"They are so cute!" Astrid cooed as Ella—or was it Emma?—smiled a huge, toothless grin.

The other baby let out an adorable trill of laughter as Quinn gently tickled her belly. Maybe helping Mrs. Halper wouldn't be so bad after all.

A huge crash came from the other room, and Mrs. Halper was off in a flash. As soon as their mom left the room, the babies' smiles were replaced by looks of sheer terror. Ella—or was it Emma?—opened her mouth and took in a deep breath. There was silence for a moment. Before Astrid and Quinn could figure out what was going on, the baby let out the type of earsplitting scream they had only heard in horror movies. Immediately the other baby joined in the wailing in a chorus of cries.

Astrid and Quinn rocked the babies and patted their backs, trying to soothe them. "What do we do?" Astrid asked franticly.

"I don't know," Quinn replied, almost having to shout over the crying babies. "Let's go find Mrs. Halper."

They walked the way Mrs. Halper had headed and found her in the kitchen. It was a large room that managed to look small and cluttered because every inch of it was covered with toys, bottles, highchairs, and brightly colored plastic bowls and plates smeared with remnants of past meals.

Mrs. Halper was kneeling down, scooping up wooden blocks and depositing them into a large bin. A toddler stood on a chair red-faced while screaming, "She knocked over my tower!"

"I'm sure it was an accident, Bryce," Mrs. Halper wearily told the angry toddler.

The little girl sitting at the table wore a mischievous smile on her face. Astrid and Quinn guessed that she was responsible for the tower.

The twins stopped screaming when they saw their mom, but they continued to whimper. Fat tears dripped from their eyes, and their bottom lips stuck out in matching pouts.

When Mrs. Halper looked up and saw the blotchy-faced babies she let out another sigh and said, "They're probably hungry. Why don't you set them in their highchairs and take the others outside to play?"

Astrid and Quinn set the twins in their bright-yellow highchairs. Emma and Ella were immediately happy again and began scooping up leftover Cheerios with their pudgy fists and shoving them into their mouths.

The angry toddler had stopped screaming. He was still standing on the chair, however, with a confused look on his face. Mrs. Halper scooped him up and set him on the floor.

"Bryce and Regan, get your shoes on and go outside," Mrs. Halper said to the little boy and his sister. She then asked, "Where's Jackson?"

"He's watching TV!" Bryce shouted as he ran out the back door without putting on his shoes. His sister, Regan, dropped the sandal she had picked up and followed her brother out the door in bare feet.

Mrs. Halper sighed, yet again, and said, "Jackson's probably in the living room. Tell him he needs to shut off the TV and go outside."

Astrid and Quinn found six-year-old Jackson sitting on the couch with his mouth slightly open as he stared blankly at the television. A cartoon they used to watch when they were younger was on. Jackson had turned the volume way up, probably to block out the sound of his screaming siblings.

"Hi, Jackson," Astrid said. "Let's shut off the TV and go outside and play, OK?"

Jackson didn't move. Quinn walked closer to the couch and said, "Hey, buddy, your mom wants you to go play outside for a little bit."

Without taking his eyes off the television, Jackson scowled and asked, "Who are you, and why are you here?"

"We're Astrid and Quinn, and we're helping your mom out today," Astrid said as she walked over to turn off the TV.

"Don't!" Jackson shouted, making Astrid and Quinn jump.

"It's time to go out and play," Astrid said again. "Come on, it will be fun!"

"Sounds stupid," Jackson grumbled.

Quinn was the oldest of four, so she knew a thing or two about handling younger kids.

"Okaaaay," she sang out as she walked slowly in front of the TV and toward the back door. "It's probably better that you stay inside. We're going to play kickball, and you probably wouldn't like it."

Jackson sat up. "I like kickball!" he shouted.

Quinn stopped and turned toward Jackson. "Oh, yeah?" she asked as she raised her eyebrows.

Jackson sat up a little more. "Yeah, and I'm really good. I could totally beat you."

Quinn moved slowly toward the door again, and without turning around she said, "Too bad we'll never find out, since you want to stay in here and watch boring old baby cartoons."

"They're not baby cartoons!" Jackson called as he jumped up and raced out. "And I'm gonna totally beat you!"

Astrid caught up to Quinn. "That was impressive," she said. "Where did you learn to do that?"

"Years of practice," Quinn replied with a smile. "I know how to handle little kids, but not crying babies. I'm glad Mrs. Halper took back the twins."

"Me, too," Astrid agreed as she scanned the backyard. "Hey, where's Bryce?"

"Is that him over there?" Quinn asked, pointing toward the back of the yard. If she squinted, she could see a small figure walking near the trees.

Bryce was standing with his back to them, facing a tree trunk. As they walked closer they saw that his pants were pulled down around his ankles. They jogged over to see what sort of trouble the little boy was up to.

"What are you doing, Bryce?" Quinn asked as she walked up behind him.

Bryce whirled around quickly and replied proudly, "Going potty."

As her shoes were splattered, Quinn jumped out of the way just in time for Astrid to run up and get her shoes soaked.

"Ew, gross!" Astrid cried out.

"Bryce!" Quinn shouted. "You need to go inside and use the bathroom if you have to go potty!"

The little boy smiled and shrugged as he pulled up his pants and ran away.

As they tried to dry their shoes in the grass, Astrid grumbled, "Maybe the crying babies would have been easier."

Three hours later Astrid and Quinn were exhausted. They were covered in finger paint, chip crumbs, and spit-up. And they had found absolutely no reason to believe Mrs. Halper took the letter. They were frustrated as they gathered their things to leave.

The four little ones were napping, and Jackson was back in front of the TV in a zombie-like trance. Mrs. Halper was showered, out of her pajamas, and looking happier than she'd been all day. "Thank you both so much for your help today. You really tuckered them out. They might sleep until dinnertime."

"You're welcome," Astrid replied wearily.

Quinn had an idea.

"It's the least we can do," she said. Astrid shot her a look that said, *Are you kidding me?* Even Mrs. Halper looked a little confused.

Quinn went on. "I mean with all the work you're doing to get the money for our schools. Astrid and I really appreciate all the time and energy you are putting in."

Astrid nodded in agreement. "Oh, yes, it means so much to us that you are going to get all of the money from the letter for us and our school!"

The smile disappeared from Mrs. Halper's face, which turned pale in an instant. "I, uh, well … "

"I'm sure you'll do whatever it takes to get the money, right?" Quinn asked, nodding.

Mrs. Halper's face went from being ghostly white to a pale shade of green. She looked more than a little nervous as she said, "Look, something has come up, and I need to back away from the campaign to get the money."

Before she could stop herself, Astrid blurted out, "But why?"

"Something has happened. You'll find out soon enough, but I can't say anything about it right now," Mrs. Halper explained. Mistaking the confused looks on Astrid's and Quinn's faces for sadness, she quickly added with forced enthusiasm, "But I'm sure the money for the schools will turn up somehow! You'll see! Maybe we'll get an anonymous donor like the water park backers did!"

"Maybe," Quinn said skeptically.

"I'm sure of it!" Mrs. Halper said as she showed them to the door. Then she asked, "Will I see you girls again tomorrow?"

CHAPTER TWELVE

Watertown University was situated at the base of Becker Mountain, which stood between Somerville and Watertown. Although it was a private school with fewer than two thousand students, the campus sprawled out across a lush, green valley. It was only a few miles from the hustle and bustle of downtown Watertown, but the tranquil and peaceful setting made it feel worlds away.

As Captain Osgood, Jace, and Rowan walked across campus toward the History Department building, they couldn't help but be impressed by their surroundings.

"Fan-cy!" Jace said as they walked along a stretch of sidewalk that was perfectly shaded by a canopy of massive oak trees. On each side they were surrounded by a combination of modern structures and well-kept, ornate old brick buildings with names such as Reavis Hall and Laurence Memorial Library.

They took their time as they walked. The school was on summer break, and the entire campus was quiet. Captain Osgood chuckled to himself as he watched the boys take in the scene. When he saw Zulauf Hall, though, the building that housed the History Department, he grew a bit more serious.

"Listen, guys, I only brought you along so I could keep an eye on you," he warned. "It makes me nervous when you conduct investigations on your own."

Rowan and Jace smiled sheepishly. Captain Osgood went on. "I need you to keep quiet while I talk to Dr. Whitaker. Aside from his fingerprints at the museum, we don't have any evidence that he may be a part of the letter's disappearance. We're just here to get a feel for what he knows and to see if he's got an alibi for when the letter was stolen."

Rowan and Jace nodded, trying to match Captain Osgood's serious expression. On the inside, though, they were ecstatic to be part of a real police investigation.

They climbed the stairs to Zulauf Hall and pulled open the heavy wood door. Silence greeted them inside the cavernous corridor. The three of them were startled when the door closed with a bang behind them. The noise echoed off the marble floor.

Captain Osgood found Dr. Whitaker's name on the directory, and they made their way to his office on the third floor. Entering a door marked "History Staff," they found an empty reception desk situated in front of a row of closed office doors. They waited a few moments before Captain Osgood called out tentatively, "Dr. Whitaker?"

A few seconds later a man in his late thirties opened one of the doors and looked around. He noticed the empty reception desk and frowned. "Is she gone again? I swear, classes end for the summer and she thinks she can make her own schedule."

Captain Osgood took a step toward the man and extended his hand. "Dr. Whitaker? I'm Captain Joel Osgood of the Somerville Police Department. I believe we have an appointment?"

The man nodded his head quickly, as if to clear it of his frustration over the missing receptionist, and shook the captain's hand. "Yes, yes," he said. "I'm Dr. Eugene Whitaker. Come on back to my office. I'd offer you something to drink, but our receptionist appears to be on another break."

"Oh, that's no problem," Captain Osgood said as he followed Dr. Whitaker to his office. He pointed to the boys and added, "This is Rowan and Jace.

They are shadowing me today to learn more about my job."

Dr. Whitaker looked back and nodded at the boys as he showed them all into his office. The room was very small, with only enough space for his desk, a couple of chairs, and a bookcase. The wall opposite the bookcase was covered with several large diplomas and a variety of certificates in ornate frames. The visitors couldn't avoid noticing them as they entered the room.

When Dr. Whitaker saw where the boys were looking, he waved his hand and laughed softly. "Oh, those! They're just my advanced degrees and certificates of achievement. No big deal. Just years of schooling and study."

He may have said "no big deal," but his voice and proud smile said otherwise. Dr. Whitaker took one last loving look at the wall and sat at his desk, facing Captain Osgood and the boys.

"What can I do for you?" he asked as he folded his arms across his chest.

"Well," Captain Osgood began, "Mrs. Partridge at the Somerville Museum says you'd been spending a lot of time there lately and I—"

Dr. Whitaker cut him off. "Has there been another discovery? Did she find more boxes for me to go through?"

They were taken aback by Dr. Whitaker's reaction. "No," Captain Osgood said slowly. "Is that why you've been at the museum so much lately? In hopes of making a discovery like Professor Higgins?"

A dark look crossed Dr. Whitaker's face at the mention of Professor Higgins. "You could say that," he said, unable to keep the annoyance out of his voice. He quickly added, "He got lucky, you know. That letter had been sitting less than twenty miles from me for all these years. It should have been me who discovered it!"

Rowan looked over at Jace and quickly raised his eyebrows. He knew that they both had the same thought: *Could Dr. Whitaker have been jealous enough of Professor Higgins to have stolen the letter?*

Captain Osgood decided to proceed cautiously. "Professor Higgins got lucky when he came across that letter."

"Lucky?" Dr. Whitaker scoffed. "A find like that defines your whole career! He'll be published in all the best journals and courted by all the top museums . . ." Dr. Whitaker trailed off, with a faraway look on his face.

Captain Osgood cleared his throat in hopes of bringing Dr. Whitaker back from his daydream about discovering an important piece of history. "Yes, well, anyway," the captain said to get his attention, "Mrs. Partridge says you came around a lot following the letter's discovery but that you haven't been in for over a week. Is that right?"

Rowan and Jace knew that meant he hadn't been in since right before the letter's disappearance.

Dr. Whitaker suddenly grew suspicious. His eyes narrowed. "You said you wanted to talk to me about the letter. What does that have to do with my visiting the museum?"

Captain Osgood kept a polite smile on his face. "I understand that you are an expert in this area. I'm simply talking to knowledgeable people about the recent find at our museum," he said. "I couldn't think of anyone more knowledgeable than you."

"Oh," Dr. Whitaker said, softening a bit at the compliment but still looking confused. "But why are you asking me about my visits to the museum? Is something going on with the letter?"

Although they had been instructed to keep quiet, Rowan spoke up. "Dr. Whitaker?" he said, squinting toward the wall of accolades. "I can't see from here. What's in that middle frame?"

Dr. Whitaker popped up and walked over to the wall. "This one?" he asked as he pointed to the framed document. "This is my certificate for perfect attendance while at Oakwood Academy."

"Oakwood Academy?" Rowan asked. "Is that a prep school?"

Dr. Whitaker leaned against his desk and looked down as he said quietly, "Actually it was my preschool."

After a long moment filled with awkward silence, Dr. Whitaker went on. "If you must know, this wall is why I've been at the museum so much lately."

"Excuse me?" said Captain Osgood. He, Jace, and Rowan were confused.

Dr. Whitaker explained, "While I've had a lot of great schooling, I don't have an achievement like the discovery Professor Higgins made on my wall. I dug through every box in that building, but I couldn't find anything in the Somerville Museum. I decided to follow Professor Higgins's lead and have been visiting small museums around the country looking for my own great find."

"So, you've been out of town for the past week or so?" Captain Osgood asked.

Dr. Whitaker nodded and said with a deep sigh, "Yes, I just got back last night. I used up my last week of vacation and didn't find a thing."

Rowan and Jace realized that with Dr. Whitaker out of town, there was no way he could have stolen the letter.

Captain Osgood stood to leave. "Thank you for your time, Dr. Whitaker. We really appreciate it."

Dr. Whitaker looked up, surprised. "Is that all?" he asked. "I didn't give you any information."

Captain Osgood smiled and said, "You've told us everything we need to know."

CHAPTER THIRTEEN

Astrid and Quinn were exhausted from their afternoon of babysitting. They dragged themselves back to the diner, where Mrs. Vega treated them to grilled-cheese sandwiches and strawberry milkshakes.

As she noisily slurped up the last of her shake, Quinn began to feel a little better. "Well, at least we learned something new," she said optimistically.

"Yeah," grumbled Astrid. "That Bryce Halper will pee just about anywhere except in a toilet. And that it's hard to get pee off of shoes."

Quinn laughed and playfully shoved Astrid. Despite her tiredness, Astrid laughed, too.

"No, silly!" Quinn said. "I would say Mrs. Halper is definitely a suspect. Didn't you think it was strange that she all of a sudden stopped trying to get the money for the schools and just about guaranteed us that the money would somehow turn up? If you ask me, she stole that letter and is going to sell it and donate the money to the school."

"If she did steal the letter, she should use the money to hire a team of babysitters for those kids!" Astrid said. She thought about what Quinn had said and added, "But if she gave that money to the schools, people would get suspicious, plus donating the money anonymously isn't Mrs. Halper's style. She'd want all the credit for something that big."

"True," Quinn said, frowning. "But she'd never be able to admit she stole the letter. Maybe she'll wait awhile and then say she found the money somehow."

"Maybe," Astrid agreed, holding her head in her hands. All of this investigating was giving her a headache. Or maybe the headache was from spending an afternoon with five kids under the age of six.

"Good morning, ladies!" Miss Coco said cheerfully. She sat next to Astrid and Quinn at the counter.

Astrid and Quinn exchanged glances.

"It's three-thirty in the afternoon, Miss Coco," Astrid replied.

"Is it?" Miss Coco asked with surprise. "I must have slept in. I was up all night catching up on some television shows I had recorded. I was way behind on my favorite program."

"What's your favorite show?" Quinn asked with interest.

"The five o'clock news," Miss Coco replied. "I like it better than the ten o'clock news. It's less depressing."

"The evening news that's on every day? With sports and weather?" Astrid asked incredulously. "You were watching old news?"

"Well, it was all new news to me," Miss Coco said as if it made perfect sense. "I hadn't seen it yet!"

Before they could say another word, a large group seated at the table behind them began arguing loudly.

"But don't you see?" said Mr. Goodwin, the owner of Goodwin's Market. "A water park will bring in more customers to the local businesses, and then the taxes we pay can help fund the schools. It's a win-win!"

Mr. Chen didn't seem convinced. "But you are assuming the water park will be a success. I don't see how that's possible with an even bigger water park less than 30 miles away. Our schools need new technology now, before our kids start to fall behind!"

Miss Coco huffed and muttered to herself, "All this arguing. I thought we'd be done with that by now."

Before Astrid and Quinn could ask Miss Coco what she meant, Jace and Rowan came into the diner, and the four kids headed upstairs to discuss the investigation.

"Bye, Miss Coco," Quinn called over her shoulder as she got up to leave.

"Bye-bye, dear," Miss Coco replied. "Oh, and don't tell me who won the Super Bowl. I'm still not caught up on my news program."

Upstairs in the Vegas' apartment, the foursome gathered around the colorful dry-erase board and exchanged what they'd learned that day. By the time they were finished, Astrid had drawn a neat line through Dr. Whitaker's name and a bright-red question mark next to Mrs. Halper's.

"Why the question mark?" Jace asked. "Do you still think Mrs. Halper might have stolen the letter?"

"Trust me, after what we saw today, I can tell you that Mrs. Halper doesn't have time to steal anything!" Quinn told them. "I don't even know how she can leave her house at all."

"That's true, but it doesn't hurt to keep her on the list for now," Astrid said. "A woman who can handle those kids is capable of anything!"

Jace laughed. He and Rowan had enjoyed Astrid and Quinn's wild stories about their afternoon with the Halper kids. "Speaking of the water park, we still don't know anything about Mr. Varner's anonymous donor," he said.

"I've found a way for us to get more information on that," Astrid said. "But it's a good-news and bad-news situation."

"What's the good news?" Rowan asked.

"Mr. Varner is having a meeting to discuss the water park plans tonight. The whole town is invited. I'm sure people will want to know more about this anonymous donor," Astrid explained.

"That sounds promising," Rowan said. "What's the bad news?"

Astrid smirked and said, "The meeting is taking place at the diner, and Mom and Dad want us to help out."

CHAPTER FOURTEEN

It seemed as if the whole town had turned out at Mick's Diner for Lance Varner's meeting about the water park. There were so many people, in fact, that the doors to the meeting room needed to be propped open. The crowd flowed out of the room and filled the diner as well.

The meeting room had been decorated as if for a beach party, with tall inflatable palm trees in the corners and cutouts of beach balls and smiling suns taped up on the walls. A banner at the far end of the room said "Wave Kingdom Jr." in gigantic yellow, red, and blue letters. The scene and mood were festive. As the residents of Somerville arrived, Mr. Varner made his way around with a huge smile on his face, shaking hands as if he were running for mayor.

Mrs. Vega was not a fan of Mr. Varner, or his water park idea, but agreed to have the meeting at Mick's once Mr. Varner said he wanted to order trayfuls of tropical-themed food and drinks for the event.

"Probably the only money we'll ever make off this silly water park," Mrs. Vega had grumbled as she cut up pineapples. As much as she didn't care for Mr. Varner, she enjoyed preparing food with a theme. She had baked iced sugar cookies that looked like beach balls and sand dollars and prepared bite-sized sandwiches cut and garnished to look like flip-flops.

Rowan, Jace, Astrid, and Quinn walked around the room carrying trays of tropical punch served in brightly colored plastic cups topped off with tiny umbrellas. Rowan stuck close to Mr. Varner, and the others kept their eyes and ears open for clues.

With almost every town resident in attendance, it didn't take long for one of them to overhear something useful to their investigation. Quinn stayed close to a certain group of women, and her persistence paid off. None of them noticed her as they began to gossip.

"Where's Stacy Halper tonight?" Mrs. Ramirez asked the other ladies. "I thought for sure she would be here trying to convince everyone to give the money from the letter to the schools."

Mrs. Studebaker pursed her lips and looked from side to side as she leaned in toward the group. "Oh, didn't you hear? She's giving up that fight."

"What?" Mrs. Reynolds was so shocked she almost spilled her beverage. "She never gives up on anything!"

"She made such a big deal about it," Mrs. Chen added. "She even convinced me to put a sign in my yard!"

Mrs. Studebaker smiled and nodded her head knowingly, clearly loving the fact that she had information the other women wanted. She paused and looked around the group. She leaned in and in a hushed voice said, "She's pregnant."

This time Mrs. Reynolds did spill. Quinn rushed over with a towel, happy to be able to get closer to the conversation.

Mrs. Chen looked unconvinced. "Are you sure? The twins just turned one. This will be, what? Baby number six?"

Quinn took her time cleaning up the spill, a little bit surprised herself. Could it be true? Poor Mrs. Halper!

"Yep," Mrs. Studebaker said with a proud nod. Nothing made her happier than being the one to break big news. "She told me herself. I ran into her at Goodwin's Market right after she found out.

I could tell something was wrong. I wanted to help, so I kept pressing her, and finally she told me. I think she was in shock herself. She's not telling anyone until she's further along. Keep it to yourselves, okay?"

The women all nodded in agreement as they looked around the room, probably trying to decide whom they were going to share the news with first. As the ladies went off in different directions to spread the gossip, Quinn signaled for Rowan, Jace, and Astrid to meet her in the kitchen.

"We can cross one more suspect off our list," Quinn said, proceeding to tell the others what she had learned.

"Are you kidding me?" Astrid asked. "No way am I ever babysitting there again!"

Rowan frowned and added, "That does make sense with what she said to you and why she would call off her fight for the money. She must have been trying to make you feel better by suggesting the money would turn up somehow."

"And you definitely would have found out later as her belly got bigger!" Jace laughed.

Just then they heard Mr. Varner's voice boom through the sound system's speakers.

"Is this thing on?" he chuckled, tapping on the microphone. "If I could get everyone's attention, I'd like to get this party started."

Rowan groaned as he rolled his eyes at Mr. Varner's cheesiness. "Well, let's hear what our last suspect has to say."

CHAPTER FIFTEEN

"Thank you all so much for coming tonight and for your enthusiasm toward Wave Kingdom Jr.!" Mr. Varner proclaimed as he pumped his fist into the air. He paused, hoping the crowd would cheer enthusiastically, but the response was mild. The local business owners who were die-hard fans of the water park cheered as if they were at a football game. But a lot of the residents had grown skeptical of Mr. Varner and his big plans. They only clapped halfheartedly. Clearly some people had come only for the food and the socializing.

"When are you going to stop talking about this water park, sell the Lincoln letter, and start building it?" shouted Mr. Rossi. There were seven children in his family, and Mr. Rossi liked the idea of having a place nearby for them to swim and have fun in the summer. His wife, however, favored spending the money on the schools. Everyone knew the couple had been arguing about it since just after the letter was found. Like most people in Somerville, though, they were getting tired of all the debating and losing enthusiasm for their causes. Mostly they just wanted things to go back to normal.

Small beads of sweat appeared on Mr. Varner's forehead. He was desperate to regain the initial enthusiasm the town had when he'd announced his plan. He knew this meeting was his last hope. "Just like you, I want to start building, but we can't get started until we raise a certain amount of money. Wave Kingdom Jr. is a great opportunity for Somerville, and I'm here to find out who is ready to invest in your town and get this project moving forward! Who's with me?"

Again the response was quiet and mild. Astrid, Quinn, Jace, and Rowan stood toward the back of the room near a table set up for food and drinks. As Mr. Varner blabbed on about how wonderful Wave Kingdom Jr. would be for Somerville, Rowan grew frustrated that no one was asking about the anonymous donor. He knew they needed some proof that would indicate that Mr. Varner had stolen the letter to use for the water park. Rowan wanted to say something but feared that since he was only twelve, Mr. Varner wouldn't take him seriously.

It was then Rowan noticed that Marcus Sloane, the young manager of Earl's Gas Station, was standing next to him. Marcus was not paying any attention to Mr. Varner whatsoever. He was too busy flirting with Jace's sister, Evie, who was filling cups with fruit punch. Suddenly, Rowan got an idea.

"Hey, Marcus," he whispered. "Kind of makes you wonder why no one is asking about the anonymous donor, doesn't it?"

Marcus hadn't been following the debate about the money and didn't have an opinion one way or the other about the water park. He had only come to the meeting for the food and to see Evie. He didn't want to appear uninformed, though, so he replied vaguely, "Yeah. That is weird."

In a voice a bit louder, to ensure that Evie would hear as well, Rowan said, "I bet no one here has the guts to ask Mr. Varner about it."

Rowan's plan worked like a charm. Marcus nodded his head earnestly and made sure Evie was listening before calling out, "What's the deal with the anonymous donor? Why would someone want to donate all that money and remain anonymous?"

Mr. Varner froze mid-sentence, his mouth and eyes wide open. The crowd, seeming tired of hearing about how great Wave Kingdom Jr. would be, was happy for the change in subject.

"Yes, well, there is an anonymous donor who has, um, agreed to put up some money for the water park, but they, uh, will only donate if the town, um, makes a commitment and agrees to spend the money from the letter on the park and invest their own money," Mr. Varner stammered.

Grumbles of displeasure arose from the crowd.

"If we give the money from the letter and there is a donor, why do we need to invest our own money, too?" Mr. Larsen called out. Others in the crowd spoke up to agree with him. Mr. Varner seemed to know the crowd was turning against him.

"I thought if we gave you the money from the letter, the donor would cover the rest?" Mr. Larsen said. "This is starting to sound shadier and shadier."

"Who, exactly, is this anonymous donor?" asked Mrs. Chen. "And how much are they donating?"

Rowan, Jace, Astrid, and Quinn exchanged glances. This was the moment they were waiting for. If Mr. Varner named a donor, it was unlikely that he had stolen the letter. Captain Osgood had arrived just in time and joined them in the back of the room.

"The donor is, um, well, very private. He doesn't want any attention drawn to himself," Mr. Varner said as he nervously rubbed the back of his neck.

The crowd grew impatient as Mr. Varner stalled. They demanded to know more about the donor. The foursome grew more convinced that Mr. Varner was the donor and had stolen the letter. After a few tense moments, Mr. Varner slumped his shoulders and in an almost inaudible voice said, "There is no donor."

A loud gasp came from the crowd, followed by a stunned silence. Mr. Varner went on, saying, "I got worried that you were losing enthusiasm for Wave Kingdom Jr. and wouldn't use the letter money to help fund it. I made up the idea of an anonymous donor so you would get excited again. Even with the money from the letter, we'd be nowhere near what would be needed to build a water park. I thought I could get outside investors interested if we had that to start with. When the investors started losing interest, I panicked and hoped you would all contribute. I'm sorry I tried to trick you."

As the residents of Somerville began booing angrily at Mr. Varner's news, Quinn turned toward the others and asked, "So now what? If there's no donor, Mr. Varner probably didn't steal the letter. We have no more suspects."

Captain Osgood frowned and said quietly, "Our only hope may be a confession."

"How do we make that happen?" asked Astrid.

"Hopefully, like this," Captain Osgood said as he headed toward the front of the room.

The crowd had closed in around Mr. Varner, angry at him for trying to trick them. He looked relieved when he saw Captain Osgood and happily handed over the microphone to the officer.

Captain Osgood clinked his glass. "Can I please have everyone's attention?" he said. "I know you are all frustrated about how we should spend any money received from the letter Professor Higgins discovered. Some of you wanted a water park, others wanted the money to go to the schools, and still others had different plans. In the end, we haven't been working very well as a community. Instead of coming together we've been fighting against each other, and I'm hoping we can change that right now."

The group settled down immediately, feeling a bit guilty for their bad behavior.

"I've got some news, and it may be a bit shocking," the captain continued cautiously. "I'm counting on everyone to remain calm so we can work together to resolve this situation."

The room was silent for a moment before Captain Osgood said, "The letter has been stolen."

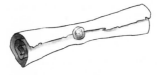

CHAPTER SIXTEEN

Captain Osgood's request for the residents to remain calm was quickly ignored. Pandemonium ensued, yet again, among the residents of Somerville.

Wild accusations flew. Friends and neighbors pointed fingers at each other. Seemingly everyone became a suspect in the eyes of others. Each of them had daydreamed about finding a treasure like that and keeping the money for themselves. They'd even had detailed discussions about what they would do with that kind of money if they didn't have to share it with the whole town. Suddenly those fantasies sounded to others like motivations to steal the letter.

"Now listen up, people!" Captain Osgood exclaimed. He had to shout into the microphone to be heard over the chaos. "This is exactly what I was hoping to avoid! If we could all settle down and discuss this like adults, I'm sure we can reason with the person who *borrowed* the letter and get it back to the museum!"

The captain's pleas went unheard. Eventually he had to put down the microphone and go to the back of the room to break up an argument that looked like it might become a fight.

Rowan, Jace, Astrid, and Quinn stood along the wall, looking to see if anyone seemed suspicious. But from what they could see, everyone looked up to no good.

"KNOCK IT OFF!" a voice boomed from the sound system. The crowd was so startled, they immediately went silent. No one was expecting what they heard next. "I stole the letter, and I'd do it again if I had to!"

While the voice was familiar, they all looked around to see if the person speaking was who they thought it was. Sure enough, at the front of the room holding the microphone stood none other than Miss Coco.

Mrs. Vega went immediately to her side, assuming the old woman was confused by all the commotion. "There, there, Miss Coco, I'm sure you didn't steal anything," said Mrs. Vega.

"I surely did!" Miss Coco replied, still shouting into the microphone. She waved her other arm around the room and explained, "And this is exactly the reason why!"

"All this," she said, waving her arm again. "All this fighting over a piece of history we should be nothing but proud of! None of you are old enough to remember any of them, but I remember my grandfather and a few of the other men and women who founded Somerville. They worked harder than you'll ever know and overcame great obstacles just so we could live in this town. If they could see you all today tearing this town apart over a little money, they'd be disgusted!"

Captain Osgood still seemed unconvinced by Miss Coco's confession. She was known to tell some pretty crazy stories. Could this be another one?

"But why?" he asked.

Miss Coco explained, "So the fighting would stop! I know how you people are these days. You all move from one thing to another in the blink of an eye, too busy to slow down and appreciate the important things. I figured you would stop fighting and forget about the letter once it was gone and move on to something else. Maybe go back to that 'bookfacing' or 'twitting' thing you're always doing. You're all too distracted by your gadgets to see the fascinating things that are right in front of you."

With tears in her eyes, she continued, "No one seemed to care about the history of this town or what went into its founding. You were willing to sell the letter without even considering what it might mean to the future residents of Somerville. Everyone was so caught up in the money. No one was showing any pride in Somerville!"

The crowd was hushed, and Mrs. Chen and Mr. Reynolds could both be seen wiping tears from their eyes.

"You're right, Miss Coco," Captain Osgood said. "But stealing is a crime, no matter the motive."

The room was quiet for a moment. People were stunned not only by Miss Coco's confession but by her moving (and completely logical) speech. No one could remember the last time she'd told a story that didn't involve something silly and nonsensical.

Mr. Reynolds broke the silence and called out, "The letter belongs to the town, right?"

Captain Osgood nodded his head and said, "Yes, it does."

"What if we all agreed not to press charges as long as she gave the letter back?" he asked. Everyone began nodding in agreement.

Captain Osgood took the microphone from Miss Coco and asked the crowd, "Show of hands. Who agrees to not press charges if Miss Coco returns the letter to the museum?"

Everyone in the room quickly raised his or her hand. Captain Osgood chuckled before saying, "Well look at that! We can all agree on something!"

The crowd cheered. People turned to each other and offered apologies and hugs. It would take a few days to admit it, but they were all relieved that the whole letter ordeal was over.

Rowan, Jace, Astrid, and Quinn made their way to the front of the room as Captain Osgood was saying to Miss Coco, "I've got to ask: How did you do it? There was no sign of a break-in."

"I didn't need to break in," Miss Coco said. "Ruth gave me a key to the museum years ago. I used to check in on things when she and Charles would go out of town. It's been so long, I bet she's forgotten I have it."

"What about the safe?" Rowan asked. "Did she tell you the combination?"

"That was a little tougher," Miss Coco admitted. "But I've known Ruth a long time, and I watch a lot of mystery programs on TV. All I had to do was try numbers I knew were important to her—birthdays, anniversaries, those types of things. Didn't take me long at all."

"Who knew you were such a good thief?" Astrid said, teasing Miss Coco.

A mischievous smile crossed the old woman's face. "There are a lot of things you don't know about me!" she said.

CHAPTER SEVENTEEN

Summer was drawing to an end. Two weeks after the hectic night at the diner, the residents of Somerville gathered once again, but this time at the museum. The mood was celebratory, and all of the arguing and debating had been put far behind them.

There were actually two occasions to celebrate that night. The first was the unveiling of the new home for the town's historic letter. Miss Coco's speech had so moved the townspeople that it was decided on the spot to keep the letter and proudly display it at the museum. A collection was taken up that very night to buy a fancy, and secure, display case.

There was even money left over, so the mayor ordered a sign to post on Highway 84. It said: "Visit the Somerville Museum! Our Town Pride Is Always on Display!" The sign had gone up a few days before, and the townspeople were surprised by the number of history buffs who traveled the highway. The museum immediately saw a noticeable increase in visitors, as did the other businesses in town.

Mrs. Partridge had returned from visiting her sister-in-law in Seattle as soon as she heard the letter had been found. She was relieved to have it back, but embarrassed by the museum's loose security. She was home less than a day before she had all of the museum's locks changed. She even suggested she might use Rex, her beloved Jack Russell terrier, as a watchdog.

"That little thing?" Mr. Vega had joked upon hearing the news. "Maybe Rex can annoy a burglar with his constant barking and jumping up and down. They'll want out of there before they have a chance to steal anything!"

Professor Higgins had returned to Somerville for the occasion as well. Just back from his vacation in Hawaii, the redheaded, fair-skinned professor was pleased that the town had decided to keep the letter in the museum. He was so pleased, in fact, that for the night, at least, he wasn't even bothered by his awful sunburn.

Several important history journals had featured Professor Higgins. He had already begun writing his book about finding historical treasures in unexpected places. Dr. Whitaker showed up and spent the evening following Professor Higgins around, hoping some of his success would rub off.

Since everyone was gathering already, it was decided that they would go ahead and celebrate some other big news at the same time—the engagement of Captain Osgood and Delilah Doherty. No one was happier about this news than Delilah's parents, who starting pestering her to set a wedding date soon after the engagement was announced.

"They've already started asking me when we're going to start our family," Delilah said. Astrid and Quinn overheard her speaking to her friends as she showed off her gorgeous ring. "It never ends!"

Miss Coco was the center of attention. She made her way around the room, chatting with folks. She was relieved that the tension from the letter was gone and was back to her usual absurd storytelling.

"Well, isn't this exciting?" she asked as she passed Jace, Quinn, Astrid, and Rowan. "History is so amazing. Things are changing and evolving all the time. The next thing you know, they'll be putting a man on the moon!"

The foursome exchanged glances and Quinn asked, "Exactly how far behind is she on those news shows?"

While everyone else was enjoying themselves, the foursome stood against the wall, all of them frowning. Captain Osgood saw them and made his way over.

"Why the long faces?" he asked as he took a huge bite of cake. Unlike the four of them, Captain Osgood wore a permanent smile on his face.

"We're frustrated that we didn't figure out that Miss Coco stole the letter," Rowan told him.

"We weren't even close. We were so convinced it was either Mrs. Halper or Mr. Varner," Jace said. "How did you know it was Miss Coco?"

Captain Osgood swallowed his bite and said, "I had no idea it was Miss Coco."

"You didn't?" Quinn asked with surprise.

"Nope," he replied.

"Then how did you know you'd get a confession when you told everyone that the letter was missing?" Astrid asked.

Captain Osgood shrugged his shoulders and said, "After meeting with Mr. P., I felt confident that the thief was a resident of Somerville. I didn't know when we'd have everyone together again, so I took a chance and I got lucky. Sometimes a little luck is just what you need to solve a mystery."

Delilah called the captain over to take some pictures. The four friends went back to leaning against the wall and pouting.

Rowan sighed deeply. "I'm not sure what I'm more upset about: the fact that we didn't figure out who the thief was, or that we have to go back to school next week."

"No kidding," Astrid said. "The only mystery to solve there will be how much homework Ms. Atwood will give us or how it is possible to stay awake through math class."

Jace was the only one excited about school starting. He had just gotten word from Mr. P. that his parents were doing well and were closer to coming home. Mr. P. said that they had agreed to let Jace and Evie stay in Somerville, since they were so happy there. Jace was looking forward to staying in one place for the time being and getting to know the kids at his new school.

"Aw, c'mon guys," he said as he turned to clap Rowan on the shoulder. "School's not so bad, and mysteries can be found any—"

He stopped speaking mid-sentence as he noticed something behind Rowan. At first he looked confused, and then shocked.

Rowan, Quinn, and Astrid turned to see what made Jace stop speaking.

"What are you looking at?" Astrid asked.

He pointed to an old black-and-white photograph hanging on the wall. It was grainy and featured a group of men wearing stoic expressions. A little placard above the photograph read: "The Founders of Somerville." Near each of the men someone had written what appeared to be their last names.

The kids found Albert Somer and Quinn's great-great grandfather, Phineas Ramsey, in the photo, but Jace's friends didn't see what had caught his attention.

Jace pointed to one of the men standing at the end of the back row, a few paces away from the other men. As they looked closer, they understood Jace's reaction.

"That guy in the photo looks exactly like Mr. P.!" Astrid exclaimed.

"It sure does," Rowan confirmed.

"So close you'd think it was an actual picture of Mr. P.!" Quinn said.

They leaned closer to get a better look. The name below the man had faded considerably. Quinn had the best view, and after a moment she called out with excitement, "It says 'Potter'!"

"As in the Potters' place?" Jace asked. "My house? The one you all thought was haunted by the infamous Potter family?"

They stood absorbing their discovery. Could it be? Could the *P* in "Mr. P." stand for "Potter"? Was he related to the mysterious family that helped settle Somerville and then disappeared without a trace?

A smile crossed Rowan's face as he said to the others, "Looks like we just found our next mystery!"

About the Author

Raised in the Chicago suburb of Hoffman Estates, Michele Jakubowski has the teachers in her life to thank for her love of reading and writing. While writing has always been a passion for Michele, she believes it is the books she has read throughout the years, and the teachers who assigned them, that have made her the storyteller she is today. Michele lives in Powell, Ohio, with her husband, John, and their children, Jack and Mia.

Glossary

alibi (AL-uh-bye)—an account of where someone was and what they were doing around the time of a crime

anonymous (uh-NON-uh-muhss)—written, done, or given by a person whose name is not known or made public

apprehend (APP-ree-hend)—to take into custody

convene (kuhn-VEEN)—gathered together

credentials (kred-EN-shuhls)—experiences that show that a person has what it takes to do a certain job

disheveled (di-SHEH-vuhld)—untidy

famished (FAM-ish-d)—extremely hungry

fruition (froo-ISH-uhn)—the completion of a plan or project

invest (in-VEST)—putting money into a project or business hoping to get more money back

monetary (MOHN-uh-tehr-ee)—something involving money

pandemonium (pan-DUH-moh-nee-uhm)—wild and noisy uproar or confusion

perpetrator (PUR-puh-TRAY-tohr)—a person who commits a crime

vague (VAYG)—unclear

validate (VAL-uh-dayt)—to find something truthful

Discussion

1. The town's residents are excited to learn that Somerville is attached to someone important. Think of your city or town. Has anything important happened there? What?

2. If your city or town suddenly had a lot of spending money, what would you want done with it? Would you want to build something big and fun, or invest it in a large project? Or would you want it saved for an emergency?

3. When the kids suspect Captain Osgood is the thief, they know they need to tell someone. But they don't know who. Who would you go to if you suspected someone you trusted of a crime?

Writing Prompts

1. The letter Professor Higgins found is one written by Abraham Lincoln to his friend, Albert J. Somer. Read some other texts about what life was like during Abraham Lincoln's time. Then write your own version of what you think his letter might have said.

2. Imagine the letter was never stolen and it had been sold. What do you think the townspeople would do with all the money? Who had the best idea of how to spend the money? Use details to support your answer. Then write your own story set in future Somerville, describing how the money affected the town and the people who live there.

3. On page 60, Rowan says Mrs. Halper once convinced him to buy cookies for a fundraiser, even though they were a kind he hated. Write an advertisement for something you don't like, trying to convince someone else that it's something they can't live without.

Solve all the SOMERVILLE Mysteries!

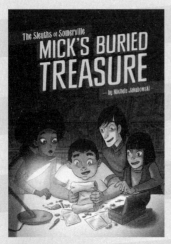

Discover more great books at
www.capstonekids.com